A NOTE TO PARENTS

Reading Aloud with Your Child

Research shows that reading books aloud is the single most valuable support parents can provide in helping children learn to read.

- Be a ham! The more enthusi⸺ you display, the more your child will enjoy the bool
- Run your finger underneath signal that the print carries
- Leave time for examining th y; encourage your child to find
- Invite your youngster to join in ... a repeated phrase in the text.
- Link up events in the book with similar events in your child's life.
- If your child asks a question, stop and answer it. The book can be a means to learning more about your child's thoughts.

Listening to Your Child Read Aloud

The support of your attention and praise is absolutely crucial to your child's continuing efforts to learn to read.

- If your child is learning to read and asks for a word, give it immediately so that the meaning of the story is not interrupted. DO NOT ask your child to sound out the word.
- On the other hand, if your child initiates the act of sounding out, don't intervene.
- If your child is reading along and makes what is called a miscue, listen for the sense of the miscue. If the word "road" is substituted for the word "street," for instance, no meaning is lost. Don't stop the reading for a correction.
- If the miscue makes no sense (for example, "horse" for "house"), ask your child to reread the sentence because you're not sure you understand what's just been read.
- Above all else, enjoy your child's growing command of print and make sure you give lots of praise. *You are your child's first teacher — and the most important one. Praise from you is critical for further risk-taking and learning.*

—Priscilla Lynch
Ph.D., New York University
Educational Consultant

To Gehn Lyon, and to all the
adventures ahead of him.
—D.B.

No part of this publication may be reproduced in whole or in part, or stored in a retrieval system, or transmitted in any form or by any means, electronic, mechanical, photocopying, recording, or otherwise, without written permission of the publisher. For information regarding permission, write to Scholastic Inc., 555 Broadway, New York, NY 10012.

Copyright © 1995 by Don Bolognese.
All rights reserved. Published by Scholastic Inc.
HELLO READER! and CARTWHEEL BOOKS are registered trademarks of Scholastic Inc.

Library of Congress Cataloging-in-Publication Data
Bolognese, Don.
Little Hawk's new name / written and illustrated by Don Bolognese.
p. cm. — (Hello Reader! Level 4)
Summary: Little Hawk comes of age through a series of events such as choosing his own horse, getting his own knife, helping with the buffalo hunt, and finally getting a new name.
ISBN 0-590-48292-0
1. Indians of North America—Great Plains—Juvenile fiction.
[1. Indians of North America—Great Plains—Fiction.]   I. Title.
II. Series.
PZ7.B63593Li   1995   93-40723
[E]—dc20   CIP
                                                                   AC

12 11 10 9 8 7 6 5 4 3 2   5 6 7 8 9/9

Printed in the U.S.A.   23

First Scholastic printing, March 1995

Little Hawk's New Name

by **Don Bolognese**

Hello Reader!—Level 4

SCHOLASTIC INC. Cartwheel ·B·O·O·K·S·®

New York Toronto London Auckland Sydney

CHAPTER 1

Little Hawk waited.
He looked across the plains.
He saw a cloud of dust.
Then he felt the ground shake.

A herd of wild horses
ran toward him.
He waved his blanket and yelled.
The horses turned.
They ran straight into the corral.

Grandfather quickly closed the gate.
Little Hawk was excited.
"Did I do well, Grandfather?" he asked.
Grandfather smiled at him.
"Now we have many new horses
for the buffalo hunt.
You may choose one for yourself."
The boy jumped onto the fence.

"There, Grandfather, that one," he said.

"Oh, my little one," Grandfather said.

"You have picked a beauty.

But be careful.

See how he paws the ground.

His spirit is great.

He will not like a man on his back,

even a small one like you."

They walked slowly to the horse.
Grandfather whispered,
"Talk to him softly.
Touch him gently."
The boy did as his grandfather said.
In a while, the horse stood perfectly still.
"Now!" Grandfather gave the command.
Little Hawk grabbed the horse's mane
and leaped onto his back.
At first, the horse was so surprised,
he did not move.
Then he raised his front legs,
whinnied, and ran straight
toward the fence.

"Hold on!" Grandfather yelled.
The boy pressed his legs hard
against the horse.
He looked up.
They were getting closer to the fence.
The horse ran faster.

Suddenly, the horse leaped up
and over the fence.
It seemed as if they were flying!

Now the horse was running again.
Little Hawk leaned over and spoke softly,
"From now on you will be
my legs and my wings."
Gently, Little Hawk turned
the horse and they rode home.

CHAPTER 2

Some time passed.
Winter was approaching.
The people needed food.
No buffalo had been found.
Grandfather said, "We must ask
the Great Spirit to lead us
to the buffalo
before the snow comes."

A huge fire was lit.
The holy men chanted. They danced.
The Great Spirit would hear them.
They would find the buffalo.
Little Hawk believed this.

Grandfather chose six braves to be scouts.
At sunrise, the scouts rode out
in different directions.
Grandfather called Little Hawk,
"We are going to look for the buffalo, too.

If the Great Spirit leads us to a herd,
your fast horse will bring the news
to our people."
Grandfather rode in front.
He looked far into the distance.
Sometimes he stopped to listen.
He got off his horse
and put his ear to the ground.
Grandfather was listening
for the thunder of the great herd.
Little Hawk thought,
Grandfather knows everything.

Several days passed.

Just before sunset on the third day,

Grandfather stopped.

He called out.

"Little Hawk, tell me.

What do you see?"

Little Hawk looked.

He squinted.

"I see clouds moving fast.

Is it a storm, Grandfather?"

Grandfather smiled, "It is the buffalo!

The Great Spirit has heard us.

Now you must hurry.

Bring everyone back here.

I will stay to watch the buffalo."

Little Hawk rode all night.
He rode the next day, too.
He stopped only to rest his horse.
Late at night, when everyone was asleep,
he reached his village.
"Buffalo! Buffalo!" Little Hawk shouted.
Everyone woke and began packing.
The women took down the teepees.
The men gathered the horses.

They hitched some to travois (trah VOY).
They were ready at dawn.
Little Hawk showed his people
which way to go.
Three days later, they found
Grandfather and the buffalo.
"We will camp here," Grandfather said.
"Tonight we will get ready
for tomorrow's hunt."

CHAPTER 3

The hunters put on buffalo skins.
Little Hawk did, too.
"I am ready, Grandfather,"
Little Hawk said.
Grandfather smiled.
"I see. And you are brave.
You brought our people here.
But you are still
too young to hunt buffalo."
Little Hawk was disappointed.

But he knew Grandfather was right.
Little Hawk's father, Gray Wolf,
had died on a buffalo hunt.
"Do not be unhappy," Grandfather said.
"You will be our lookout."

Slowly, very slowly, the hunters
approached the buffalo.
Little Hawk watched from a hill.
His job was to signal the hunters
when the herd began to move.
He made a small fire and waited.
The hunters circled the buffalo.

They were very close.

Some buffalo stopped eating.

Little Hawk got ready.

Soon the herd began to move.

Little Hawk put his robe

over the fire, then took it away.

A white puff of smoke went up.

The hunters saw it.
They raised their bows
and aimed their arrows.

The buffalo tried to run away.

But the horses stayed close to them.

Arrow after arrow flew into the herd.

Many buffalo fell.

When their arrows were gone,

the hunters used their lances.

The herd kept running.

Finally, the hunters were done.

Little Hawk rode down the hill
to meet Grandfather.
"A great hunt, my little one,"
Grandfather said.
Little Hawk was glad.
He said, "The Great Spirit is good,
Grandfather."

Now the tribe had
food to eat and
warm buffalo robes to wear
during the winter.
They had extra buffalo hides
to trade, too.
In the spring, Grandfather would go
to the great meeting place,
where the tribes and the white men
traded with each other.
This year, Little Hawk
would go with Grandfather
for the very first time.

CHAPTER 4

In the spring, Grandfather and Little Hawk
rode to the meeting place.
Little Hawk saw many people
from different tribes.
One man kept looking at him.
The man rode up to Little Hawk.
He pointed to Little Hawk's horse,
then to his own furs.
"What does he want, Grandfather?"
Little Hawk asked.
"He wants your horse.
He will give you his furs,"
Grandfather answered.
"I don't want to trade," said the boy.
The man took off his vest.
He held it out.
Again, Little Hawk said no.
This time the man got angry.
He rode away.

Little Hawk saw some hairy-faced men.
Their smell was strong.
He stared. "Who are they?" he asked.
Grandfather smiled.
"They are white men," he answered,
"who live in the mountains where
they trap and hunt.

Come, Little Hawk, let us see
what there is to trade."
Little Hawk saw many things—
colored cloth, beads, steel knives.
Grandfather traded a stack of hides
for two knives.
"One for you, little one," he said.
"Thank you, Grandfather,"
Little Hawk answered proudly.

The next day, Grandfather
visited friends from another tribe.
Little Hawk rode around
looking at all the people.
He watched games and contests,
even horse races.
As he passed two mountain men,
one spoke to him,
"That is a fine horse you have, boy.

I'll bet he's fast, too."
"He is, he is," said Little Hawk.
"We think he can outrun
any horse here," said
the mountain man.
And his friend agreed.
"See those fellows?" He pointed
to three braves on horseback.
"If you race them, these are yours."
He held a string of beads
and a set of tiny silver bells.
Little Hawk knew that Mother and
Little Sister would like them.
"Come on, boy. Just a little run
and these are yours, win or lose."
"How far?" Little Hawk asked.
"From here to that big spruce tree
and back," said the mountain man.
He waved to the braves.
They rode over.

One was the man who had wanted
to trade for Little Hawk's horse.
One of the mountain men shouted,
"Get ready—go!"
Little Hawk's horse took the lead.
But two of the riders caught up
with him at the turn.

They pushed Little Hawk's horse
to the side.
A fallen tree was in the way.
But Little Hawk's horse
jumped right over it.
Now, no one could catch up
to Little Hawk.

The mountain men were yelling,
"We won, we won!"
Little Hawk shouted, "Grandfather,
did you see? I won!"
Grandfather looked at the men
who had lost.
They were giving their furs
to the mountain men.

"Yes," Grandfather said. "You won.
But they lost their furs.
They are angry.
Come now. Let us go to our camp.
We will have to leave at dawn."

CHAPTER 5

"Little Hawk, wake up.
A storm is coming."
Grandfather and Little Hawk
mounted their horses and rode out.
By afternoon, snow began to fall.
Little Hawk heard something.
He looked back.
"Grandfather, look!" he cried.

Three riders were following them.

Little Hawk was scared.

"This is bad," Grandfather said.

"Those are the men you beat in the race.

They want your horse.

Go! Quickly! Get away!

I will hold them off."

"But, Grandfather," Little Hawk cried.

"I said, 'Go!' Now!" Grandfather shouted.

He slapped Little Hawk's horse hard.

The horse ran.
Little Hawk held on and rode.
Night came. The storm ended.
Little Hawk stopped.
He looked back at his tracks.
He felt afraid and angry.
I cannot leave Grandfather,
he thought. *I must go back.*

Slowly he rode back over his trail.
He came to a place
where there were many hoofprints.
"This is where Grandfather fought,"
he said to himself.
He followed the horse tracks.

He rode a long way.
Then he saw a fire.
He climbed down from his horse
and crawled closer.
Grandfather was tied up!
Little Hawk saw that the men who
captured Grandfather were asleep.
Silently, he crept to their ponies.
He tied all the reins to one rope.

He checked his knife
and climbed back on his horse.
He spoke softly in his ear.
"Those men didn't think
we would come back for Grandfather.
We'll surprise them!"

They galloped to
Grandfather's side.
Little Hawk swung down
from his horse and
cut Grandfather free.
The men woke up.
Grandfather and Little Hawk
jumped on the horse,
but the men blocked their path.
Little Hawk yelled,
"Hold on, Grandfather!"
They ran toward the men.
The horse leaped and flew over them.
"Heeyah!" cried Grandfather
as he grabbed a headdress.

Little Hawk raced to the ponies
and picked up the lead rope.
"Here, Grandfather. Take this.
They can't follow us now," he shouted.
When they were safe,
Grandfather got on his own horse.
After a while, he spoke.
"Little Hawk, you did not obey me.
But, I forgive you."
"Thank you, Grandfather,"
Little Hawk answered.

Grandfather spoke again,
"You did a great thing.
You are not a boy anymore.
Now you are a brave.
Your story will be told
many times around our campfires."

Grandfather took off his necklace.
"This was to be your father's,"
he said, "but now it is yours.
From this time on,
you will be called
He-Who-Jumps-Over-Everyone."
The young brave with the new name
was too happy to speak.